How Do You
Know My Name?

How Do You Know My Name?

Mia Collins

To order additional copies of this book, contact:
Xlibris
UK TFN: 0800 0148620 (Toll Free inside the UK)
UK Local: (02) 0369 56328 (+44 20 3695 6328 from outside the UK)
www.Xlibrispublishing.co.uk
Orders@Xlibrispublishing.co.uk
857732

How Do You Know My Name?

On a stagnant summer day the air is dry and still, bearing the heat wave from this claustrophobic place as I sit in the dr's waiting room for my appointment. e time is going incredibly slow, it's too hot even with a small fan that was as futile as a chocolate fireguard, trying to sit still and not writhe too much and certainly didn't wish to make eye contact with others sitting across the room. I hear the receptionist in the other room gossiping to her colleague about her nail salon appointment then I feel myself zoning out as I peer around the room to read the gruesome diseases they have on posters to pass the time and mind numbing boredom I was contemplating just leaving and not bothering at all.

My mind wandered o f to the wistful thoughts of tonight, it's Friday, I've already dropped the children at my family's house. As a result I'm free to hit the town, but just as my mind wanders to something exciting the ping of my name scrolled across the digital screen ~'Tabitha Mckenzie Dr Walker Room 2.' Here I go at last I almost forget what I was waiting for the last hr, what was he doing with the last patient. I'm always in and out in five minutes and people in front of me seem to be in there for forty five mins at least.

I walk along the short corridor perplexed to what he wants me in for, the smell of sterile cleaning is sickly and the atmosphere is worse than being in church as a small child zoning out to another place to block the feeling of wanting to leave again.

Upon entering the room I'm greeted with a grinning GP who always appears sanguine, perhaps because he's always o f on sabbatical swanning around the world on those gigantic cruise ships. He was sitting in his swivel chair as I walked in and sat down, he leaned forward and grins with warmth, he was a welcoming friendly man, he had a gentleness about him and he made me feel comfortable. About 5'9" with a balding head probably coming into his sixties by now and of slim build, with cold blue eyes, but not foreboding ~ I digress, he sits me down and asks me straight out:

"We called you in, "….he pauses to turn and grabs a dictaphone as he holds it out no words needed he's made it clear he's recording. I was used to this dr and by this point we had a trust. "We are concerned about the extent of your historical injuries and how you got them, can you enlighten me… .or are you not ready to talk about this ? Hmm, he sighs as I stare at him perplexed to what he's trying to ask me. "Sorry, have I walked into the wrong room? " was my response; 'we're very concerned that your injuries were so severe we had no choice but to diagnose Amnesia, I had to go to court on your behalf because you didn't remember'_but it's ok I don't think it's come back to you, perhaps it won't…(*he's muttering something gobbledygook to me?*)

Still wondering what he is on about I start spilling out questions, can you enlighten me to what has happened ? He wouldn't give me information but told me this much. ~' e extent of your head injury showed a hole in your skull and a fracture the equivalent of a car crash we were informed a hammer did this damage,' as he looks at me for an answer, I have a blank look on my face *nothing* ...he drones on I almost drift o f, 'Your insides are so damaged you will need plastic surgery to repair it was too bad to heal by itself so one day if you wish to face this'_we can help with that if you like ? ...it would have healed but badly, unfortunately you'll need to address this down the line after you finish having children. "Gee thanks," with even more uncertainty I thought. 'We believe you had a heart attack, we know you were given CPR and you stopped breathing.' "Anything"~ he asks ? "a, *No idea*' I shrug and again completely mystified. But curious, I'm not being given enough information by him to make a complete picture. At this point He looks back to his computer, adding notes.

"WAIT"? Listen with great respect...I'm pretty sure if this had happened to me I'd know about it ? He carried on divulging this confidential information from his list. 'We believe you were gang raped while you were unconscious. is was long enough to now be able to tell you... I didn't tell you sooner because we didnt want you to reject the baby women who've been raped reject their rape babies but now she's nine I thought you'd be ready to talk?' *None of this is sinking in* ~"We made a grave mistake because you were unable to make a statement in court due to your Amnesia, it wasn't until nine months later we realized and with deep regret new evidence/DNA came that one of the older men who had clearly lied had fathered your child. " I'm very sorry to be having to bring this up but he had a delayed prison sentence but justice was done on your behalf nevertheless.

I lean forward to try to hear him better as i'm bewildered. As I pipe up a response 'I'm sorry but I believe you are talking to the wrong woman thats ridiculous trust me if I was raped I'd kill them, or they'd be left with irreversable scars for life, and you shouldn't be telling me someone else's private files_!'

He leans back, switching o f his dictaphone with a deep sigh of disappointment. He pulls my chair towards him, as he leans in touching my knees in a form of comfort which to me felt odd, not really a fan of contact with men I'm not in a relationship with. It feels intimate so I leaned back "is that all ?" We did our best, your injuries and your grandmother told us you were in a coma for two weeks, we couldn't find you or your child? She told us about how she came each day to administer drops of water and let it trickle down to keep you alive and how your family was waiting for you to die, they thought you were better o f dead which adds torture to facts.

Your son was taken by your aunts and watched until you were physically well again. " Do you remember this?"~ Err no? We don't agree with not calling the police but it appears you were gravely let down by them but the judge saw through their lies in court.

You're lucky to be alive and having memory loss is ok, as long as you feel you're ok he questioned, concerned about the look of confusion on my face. Nothing he said rang a bell whatsoever.

It appears your friends aren't very nice, he piped up to say that last thing.. 'What? -I replied. Who?' I asked, but no facts were given, still none the wiser.

I thought to myself this feels weird is he ok having some sorta last min life crisis or what. "One last thing he pipes up, just as I was about to get up from my seat … .I've sent your files... I decided to do this for you so one day when you're ready you can get them in paper form at New Highfield Hospital. ey've been listed and stored never to be destroyed so you can request them if you wish to do so.. 'ok ?' Confused by this, I still have no idea what he's trying to say. I immediately brush aside this odd meeting convinced there's a big mix up.

As I left the room I quickly had thoughts of what I would wear tonight. I was unable to hold onto things for too long at this point in my life and would quickly be able to carry on in that moment every day.

I'm so looking forward to a night out and soon this weird conversion was forgotten about. [literally.] Stepping out into the fresh air of that stu fy humid building, the air was hot as I walked to my car. I was already calling my date for later on, "Hi, so where are you taking me tonight, I can't wait?".... with a big grin on my face all the way home music blaring, oh I'm already in the mood feeling confident that my new dress and shoes were going to look amazing. ere was nothing, no cued recall, nothing anyone could have done to reach what was buried deep, how would I have been able to retrieve something that happened while I was unconscious?

Ĩf I can't remember any point dwelling on it, move on..

Chapter One

Tabithas Diary:
Present time, my child is an adult, emendation: …. All my children are adults apart from one who's a teenager.

Life's been amazing, but as I reminisce my life began flashing before my eyes on a daily basis,~ why was my mind wandering to the past involuntarily so much? I was bewildered by what some of the memories were, some are amazing and some are alarming. is was clearly apparent; it was a mild form of PTSD so I believed.

I had brushed aside the conversation about Amnesia all those years ago. However, I figured it would never resurface as hard as I try, nothing at all sprang to my mind but the present time and being incredibly busy with my family, I was happy I was living the dream, wanting for nothing, always content and raised to be humble about material items. In spite of that everything was hunky dory one didn't need much or want more than I had except perhaps the dream to own my own home one day, so I can leave my children a roof over their head.

The ups and downs, they didn't nickname me cat woman for no reason. Apart from the eye liner which made the eyes pop. I always landed on my feet or high heels should I say, this confidence I had of self love was what carried me forward all my life but made me enemies along the way. Other people call it arrogant, I called it tenderness/self love. I would always in my youth be well turned out unless it was a school run then yea who had time for that pull back the hair and get the sunglasses out and hope I didn't see anyone to stop and chat until I had time to go home and shower and fix my confidence back in one piece. at was nothing short of a small miracle: the power of makeup and hair curlers and a decent pair of jeans. Now I will say this, River Island was the jeans to die for. I could throw on any clothing in my younger days and rock it.

I don't feel that way these days. Old age strips away any confidence that you have as a youth to an extent, I feel my mind is now taking over the body and focusing on work instead of running around raising small children. Life became a lot simpler all of a sudden.

I look in the mirror as I wonder who this woman is looking back at me and why am I always tired these days. ere was a time I'd be doing a hundred press ups followed by a hundred sit ups in my younger days and some in between if I felt restless I'd pop to the gym if I had time. Insecurities did not exist. I don't think that's a bad thing in hindsight. I wish I still felt it but I'm content nevertheless. I've great friends along with my family in Ireland whom I chat to here and there to catch up, Iceland too my family members dwell.

My life has been something of a small miracle with a twisted fate of evil along the way of a grave misjustice of criminals and drug dealers which I have no empathy for those who take that road and choose to be criminally driven. Crooked cops and thank god for a intelligent GP who did the rape swabs and recorded the skull injury and its extent, the attack had stopped my heart once and the upon awakening a naturally induced coma i'd experienced a elephant sitting on my chest metaphorically speaking, to be told my heart attack had left scaring in on my heart. It wasn't until years passed someone slipped up and bragged they'd spiked my drink *[they even boasted about murders]* with four and half grams of heroin in a half pint drink handed to me by a bar man who mistook me for a policewoman undercover, as his paranoid mind wondered thinking being a stranger in town I was CID looking to find him dealing copious amounts of drugs from his money laundering businesses. *If the shoe fits, wear it.* I chose to not be told the identities of said criminals that way I can't be blamed if fate catches up with them it's nothing to do with me but karma itself.

Within the powers of recall my memories that have begun to surface over the last five years, like a raindrop one at a time each day joining together to create a picture just like a jigsaw of memoirs have finally settled and now I remember who I used to be, who I used to know and places I've seen that were forgotten. *~Amnesia.*

I used to say I've never done this. I've never done that, talking about visiting places and experiencing life itself. I always thought I led a sheltered life, but little did I know what was about to unfold.

I recall my nan teaching me how to spell my name all over again in my twenties. She is usually bad tempered but now she was caring, her worry was beyond it as she thought she was saying goodbye to me, she knew I could die at anypoint point. She was a tiny 5ft tall strong minded outspoken republican who was originally from Ireland so she wasn't estranged to hard work or poverty but proud of who she was and where she came from, she had strong catholic morels and never lowered herself to be anything but upper class in her ways nevertheless. She once had jet black shiny hair straight all the way down her back and her beauty was outstanding still even though she was now a pensioner you could see who was once underneath the now beginning to gray hair, in fact hardly much gray she was lucky, but her hair now a shorter bob.

A large skull fracture had been to the left side over the ear, I recalled placing my finger into a hole in my head blood dripping down my cheek and a policeman saying you need to go to hospital, little did I recall this was attack three of over twelve in total followed by eleven other minor attacks over a period of thirty one years. My memory was scatty but there once was a time I was told I had a photographic memory which was mostly lost now. *Apparent Stalking.*

What confused me the most at first was some memories were good some were bad, I didn't understand why I was getting both but unbeknown to me this was my life coming back to me everything forgotten is now back.

Upon requesting help too soon from my new dr. he was reluctant to help, he dismissed and misdiagnosed me due to

I had only told him one snippet of my story at the beginning while I was reaching out to ask what it was and why I had these memories which felt brand new. Little did I realize they were very real life experiences and now I had to go face them alone. Little was my dr aware he'd lost all my medical files from the past so how could he diagnose correctly now?

My entire life begins to unfold and slowly remember who I am and who Iwas:

Chapter Two

I'm sitting alone. It's a quiet evening now. I've been experiencing flashbacks for five years by this point so every one of them makes sense, sometimes they're hard to place in an orderly manner but excessively clear this was who I was, self displaying my life beforehand.

Along this road called life you learn who the gaslighters are, when you begin to reach out and ask people about the past they either cover up and lie, but this enables me the wean out the real friends who will be honest telling you yes thats what happened and even help fill in the blanks which is extremely reassuring. I no longer have any use for narcissists intertwined in my life, so they were easy to wean from.

The beginning

~Flash back~

I'm four years old, it's a wintry morning around Nine irty am. I guess this time as Mass is usually around Ten am. We were on our way to church, the catholic church which was two miles away in the next joining town. I'm sitting on the back of a bike in a child's seat, all I have on is a red rain pullover, thin anorak, a vest and a jumper, the hoods up it's misty cold weather, my hands are frozen, I recall seeing them red as I tried to cover them with the sleeve of the very thin anorak. I was a tiny, slim built child, slightly dark skinned with dark brown straight hair with a fringe. I had no self awareness at that time only needing comfort and nourishment, the simpler times. I'm feeling totally sorrowful for myself, but I've learned to numb myself from boredom. I just look at the sights on each side, as we pass the fields I stare at the cows as they look back at me. Oh' I hated church. I recall the footpegs were broken on my seat on the back of the bike so I had to keep my legs away from the wheels so as not to get tangled in the spokes below. is had happened before so my fear was intelligence. I remember how much this hurt. As the rain mists down a car pulls alongside us heading down the main road which felt like it went on forever even though it was just two miles but to me at age four this road was eternal.

The passengers window winds down and a lady's head pops out she leans over arms out friendly and wanting to help she could see I was frozen and o fered to take me to church for them and wait in the warm until they arrived as she explained she goes to the same church every sunday and sees us there often and explained her mother is friends with my grandmother. My aunt was stern and dismissed her o fer as she was a stranger and consequently didn't want to risk letting me go o f with strangers which was wise.

She said it's ok I understand but appeared insulted in hindsight. She wore a smart church crown hat and wore a skirt suit smartly dressed as every does for church on sundays. Her hair was dark, she looked around thirty ish not that i'd figure that out at age four but at a guess.

There was a man driving but unsure if this was husband or her driver. As the car began to pull away a young boy older than myself by about nine years, with longish brown hair for a boy I found it odd but it was said (*if Jesus had long hair why cant boys?*) I couldn't count the days of course but I recall him being bigger than me. He kneeled up in the back seat and peered out the back window sticking his tongue out at me.

This made me cry, why was he so mean? He spun around and sat down all of a sudden with such a whip that it appeared he was getting a hard smack, and he jumped arms and legs up in a defensive manner which I coiled to see as I was up high looking down into the car. Not accustomed to any form of violence myself as I was spoiled wrapped in cotton wool and loved. I had a protected life as a child so innocently naive.

The following summer soon came around and this boy and I made friends and subsequently taught me to ride a bike. Encouraging me to just get on he held onto my seat until I was o f and boy was I o f, I had it first try, he was di ferent this time much kinder and patient. Maybe he realized he shouldn't be mean to little girls. He has long hair, he is slim built, not very tall for his age and most definitely immature but kind to me and patient for someone his age. He would get spooked easily and run o f all of a sudden nervous. I found this odd to be honest why he was so jumpy. is lad was easily tanned but I don't think he was as dark as me naturally, but all sun kissed instead. Brown eyes and a chubby cheek look but not overweight.

Jonny's grandparents [both sides]were from my village so he was there a lot during summer breaks.

As time went by we became friends, a lot of us in fact not just myself but i'm speaking from my own point of view. Our grandmothers would be standing in the school bus stop chatting and joking bringing the world to rights .. Her name was Victoria but she liked to be called Vicky. She had red hair graying and wore glasses, tall, freckles, she would lift her chin up as high as she could like she was looking to the sky but just in deep thought to reply. On other days Sometimes if my nan had to go out I'd stay around Jonny's grandparents for a day and play with his sisters Sassie and Sarah, so at di ferent times and di ferent years sometimes we'd all play in the garden. We avoided the bee hives their grandfather kept in his very large garden which at times felt like a maze navigating our way around it to find the shed where we often played dens. I think there were around eight, but I can't recall if I ever counted them.

His name was Jonny but he liked his nan to call him Andrew in play. at was weird. So at teatime we would be hanging out in the field next door to their house and she would call out ANDREW? It only lasted one summer and he never used this name again. He'd run into his grandparents after being dropped o f, his mother was bad tempered. She scared me. *is is the same lady from the car when Iwas four who offered us a kind lift.* I would stay back but she would turn and say 'hello Tabitha, how are you,'?_spoken nicely, this was freaky. I was still afraid of her as I had seen her swipe Jonny in church a few times. He once made me laugh across the aisle and disturbed the priest giving his sermon. She gave him a few whacks and as I witnessed him running out of church. I saw him ducking many times over the years as she threw or swiped for him as he ran in doors. She was strict. She wasn't tall but her personality was big. But over the years she seemed to mellow into a more friendly old lady, I recall her talking to me a lot oddly now. I guess everyone was a stranger for a long time. I wasn't used to that kinda parenting. *Not everything was lost, some odd memories remained which is why it was easy to carry on.*

In time as my memories began to resurface, I recall I'm a little older playing kiss chase, Jonny was the first boy to kiss my cheek which shocked me. ere was innocent moments growing up we hang out go conker collecting he used to wear a eye patch, I didn't realize it was for his lazy eye, and then he explained it to me but vaguely, I even heartlessly took the mick subsequently he took o fense, at that he took it o f putting the patch in his jean pocket giving me a stern look of_I hurt his feelings. I wasn't quite at the age yet of being compassionate but I wasn't mean then. Not on purpose anyway.

He would appear over the years as he'd always come and stayed with his grandparents while both his parents worked. ey couldn't leave the children alone during the summer holidays. is became less as they got older. I only saw Jonny. e girls had grown up enough to stay home in london.

As I grew older he began to look upon me di ferently, keener, what's the term I'm looking for? *Growing up* .... I bumped into again when I was fifteen, we're sitting in a den a hedge ok, he places his arm around me leans in to kiss me one on the cheek one of the corner of the lips, I'm not yet experienced to make out to which I replied "Im a virgin "! which to my horror is the most embarrassing thing to have said. I felt like the ground could have swallowed me up. He was now looking thinner than he had years before his puppy fat had fallen o f and he was beginning to look handsome but in a girly way as he had the long hair. A year later when I'm sixteen he saw me in a club we both used to sneak into on the air base, I turned around and caught him staring. He looked away then back and made a hand gesture, he appeared to be having inner thoughts of lust~" no, no, you're hot!, no no,.. you're like a little sister to me no",.. At that he turned heels and ran but looked back with a gleam in his eye of which with that he of course retreated. He was soon back up on the stage dancing with me, standing still in those days he didn't like to dance. We ended the night with a YMCA dance on stage but I mashed it up big time and couldn't keep up. Furthermore we danced for years to come until my legs couldn't dance any more and for fits of laughter of being spun in circles, even barn dances he made sure I was the one flying round like a helicopter but I can't recall the name of the dance. *yet.*

It wasn't long before I'm seventeen. At this stage he asked me out on an o ficial date. He sent a car to collect me. is date went wrong. I upset him. I wasn't ready for what he was o fering. I wasn't ready to be involved, and he was upset I hadn't dressed up so he left in a hu f saying he can't take me to posh restaurant in jeans, he hasn't made it clear we were going there as he said meet at a pub so I dressed down for said pub was a biker bar sorta ga f. He sent a car to take me home and I hated his letchy driver. But reminiscing to that night, Jonny didn't give up he asked me what is it you want to do your dreams, every dream I told him he made it happen, I'd say never been bowling so he took me bowling, I've never been to a drive in cinema so he took me to a drive through cinema, I would love to see Paris, he took me to Paris to the Ei fel Tower, [*there and then*] including the Tate Gallery and many other days and nights happened seaside trips.. is went on for years. By this point he was an A class movie star bringing in millions so the treats were at an easy reach for him but he didn't forget his grounding not yet anyway. He would find me and beg me not to tell my friends who he was or that he was there dragging me round a hidden corner hiding to say hello. I had to carry this secret from my family too.

Our friendship was close like best friends at one stage but we didn't see each other often. He was always working away and in return it would all start up again, hanging out going out. Over a long period of years he would keep bumping into one another. I always said We were like the movie {e Way We Were} . I said once I feel one day when we are old we will bump into each other to remember all the way back to our childhood. Unbeknown to me this was about to all change and he would be wiped from my memory and some other friends along with it too who were connected when he and I were out together. I guess an entire piece was missing like taking away a capacitor to a tv unit to make it start up and work, like pieces missing from a harddrive so it will no longer defrag.

Over a period of thirty one years he would try so hard to make me remember him but he was a stranger all over again every time we met and I went home to sleep he was gone the next morning a blank canvas. How could this be? He showed me photos, he showed me ID but nothing (after twenty six years I started to recall but it was thirty one years before any of it made sense.) It didn't a fect me so much as he was more confused than I, I knew nothing, he was a stranger to me in my eyes by this point so his perplexed look upon his face accompanied by sad eyes that I know longer knew who he was.

Jonny kept turning up to my hospital appointments over the years. I recall him screaming and crying in the drs. Why doesn't she remember me? Can we get a second opinion ? To which no avail was given or o fer of help the drs ignored it all because I was cognitive functioning day to day they weren't aware only Jonny knew nobody else helped, only him !

Even more perplexing is he was there at many of my babies scans and births, even holding my hand to cut the cord. He stayed three days feeding my baby while I was in hospital. I thought he was just a volunteer. I had no idea what he was talking about each time we met.

He would often say remember me, remember please, he wrote me letters, he painted me a baby elephant and wrote on the back all the places we had been together recently. It began to get very dark when I was forced to go for an abortion and "this baby was his" ! . I remember him screaming and crying at the hospital like he thought I knew it was his but I had nothing of the nts we spent together no longer was he there but just a stranger all over again. All I know is I didn't want this abortion I was forced into it, threatened and beaten to the point of agony by an ambulance and told if I don't get rid they'll punch it from my stomach. *I feared for my life and my unborn child's life.*

I felt this baby was already dead inside me after the beating I took and the bleeding I had the next morning of how much agony that baby had to endure was so cruel and unfair how it su fered. I'm Bleeding from the beating, a police lady came and took photos of the heel marks on my belly and this baby had been kicking and doing summersaults. I could feel it at twelve and a half weeks moving .. it was incredibly energetic more than any of the rest it wanted to live but it had that taken from it. I wish I had been strong enough to fight from these people, making me go down that road in fear of my life. ey came to my house every day to tell me to get rid of it. " e father hates you." they would say all kinds of unkind taunts and my mind wasn't strong enough to fight their gaslighting. It ground me down that they'd never go away if I didn't agree as they demanded. e child was strong and wanted to live but they took this from me which I will never forgive.

-_As time went by once again, there was nothing he could say or do to make my mind recall any of it. It was all wiped completely .. until now. I never told him I remember him to this day. He as far as I'm aware doesn't know I'm back ! *I think it's best now to leave it that way.* I never had the chance to tell him about the last baby, oddly he came to my house and tried to tell me I was pregnant again, he knew, although I never confirmed it until I lost it, that's how I found out I was growing baby number six... I miscarried at three and half months. is perfectly little formed baby inside its sack still attached to the placenta all came away in one piece which deeply upset me. I didn't tell anyone except the midwife, it made no sense I didn't recall being with him at the hospital he came to visit me and that's when we conceived that child. Even the midwife tried to ask me about Jonny. She'd heard he was at the hospital with me. All I could do was look at her saying "I don't know what you mean who ?" Too much pain has gone between us. ~ *ere's no looking back. What would be the point? I couldn't remember him anyway !*

When memories come back it's one thing to recall people you'd forgotten but to recall the lovers you had were Celebrities and Royals is something else entirley !

Chapter Three

Years before the loss of memory as Jonny and I walked down a country lane near my caravan close to where I was living at that time, or perhaps close by, this one was still rusty. I couldn't place a time period. I just know I was young between seventeen and twenty two. It's a big time period but it will come later. I've learnt to trust memories to come back in more detail down the line. e blistering sun from above on this heatwave of a summer's day as often these walks we shared were always fun, we walked and talked for hours drinking beers/lager, I can't recall which brand, anything we could have got our hands on. ose kinds of details don't seem important enough to hold onto. We had walked too far, at this point Jonny perks up and turns heel pointing back in the other direction. It's this way and I'm wondering where we're going by this point.. Always a surprise with him *you won't know until you get there.* we got carried away in conversation god knows what we wa fled on about in those days, cars bikes and nights out perhaps. We walked over a little bridge the sign read " Weak Bridge"! I said "oh stop, we better go over one at a time you're a lump" but I was laughing too much. His face was shocked and it took him a moment to get it or in hindsight perhaps he wasn't amused. By this point he wasn't bad looking but still a bit of a scruff for my liking but he looked better in baggy jeans than in suit trousers he was skinny for a man. He needed more muscle. We turned back and walked towards this beautiful house. e garden wall was low but the drop on the other side got lower as you walked along so we could climb in. Jonny suddenly jumps this wall "come on" beckoning me to follow,~'I'm not climbing in someone's garden that's trespassing.' He shouts: 'come now' ..*in a hurry.* God he's impatient I thought. So I clamber over but fear the consequences of being caught. is was Charlie lynch's house, Charlie was also a big movie star in fact bigger than Jonny at this stage and his films were box o fice hits. At this walking down the path to the back door we walked inside and were not aware at this point his wife was inside. She said 'he's not here Jonny', but I had followed him inside by this point. Jonny takes me by the arm and points down to look at the floor and there's Charlie swimming under a glass floor with the fishes.~"What the hell am I seeing here?"I ask.. Omg this is the funniest thing I've ever seen. But I'm mesmerized by this. Jonny gets panicked and shouts for him to come out he feared he'd drown.. Charlie was doing the frog stroke and it was hilarious. A few moments later he emerges with a towel drying his hair as he enters the living room, "I've been drinking all day, *laughs*, thought I'd have a bit of fun was good wasn't it?" he says.. Jonny and I were too pissed to respond, well actually speaking for myself I can't keep up with him I was always asleep first. Used to be in those days when partying was our middle name.

When I first set eyes on Charlie I was instantly attracted to him but he didnt notice me in hindsight in that way I don't think so anyway. He was so handsome, nice body, dark neatly cut hair and gorgeous eyes that pinned to you with depth of sex appeal, better build, more manly and stronger than Jonny, the kinda build who could take you in his arms and swoop you up. Charlie's garden was stunning, full of tropical and all kinds of plants with a stream; or perhaps it's a large pond as there's a water mill on the side of the house keeping the water running for the fish below his living room floor. As we sat on the patio furniture outside, all Charlie kept saying was 'I've had two showers re gelled my hair and I can still smell fish'~ this was hilarious. He just was so self bothered by himself smelling you had to be there to understand the funniness of this.

I recall Charlie liking his fish he was messing around one evening in a local pub bringing me drinks all nt. He introduced me to his father, Martin lynch. *Martin was even bigger than the other two as fame was to have it known all around the world as a real big shot.* As I walked over I went to shake his hand, pleased to meet you, ~"oh no, the pleasure is all mine!" as he lets o f a

Loud echo of laughter. Martin had a firm handshake but genial with me. At this point Jonny is sitting at the same table and pipes up. Hey, remember me?...."No, !" I replied and they laughed but Jonny wasn't happy.

I could sense he thought I was pulling his leg but nothing was there at all he looked like a total stranger. He still couldn't figure out why I can't recall him everytime we meet. To a point he'd sometimes get angry he was convinced I was doing it on purpose but that wasn't the case. Not by a long shot. e damage was done to the brain the day the attack.

Further back:

As the memories flood my mind…From hanging around by Georgo Partin's [Georgo was a top shot producer manager, a billionaire] pool in his back garden to watching his son play live in a band, over hearing him say "I know he's my son but he hasn't got it", .. to having a sweet moment meeting Paul Harty[famous artist] and Jason Dingo [a famous singer] he was fairly handsome actually, all these people being friends in all in the same industry so it's inevitable to meet them all if you wonder why. I met him a few brief times and he introduced himself because he would hang out at Jonny's place. *they were all Actors or singers. How was I entwined with this life?* I just knew there was more to remember.

One evening Jonny spots me out and about in town having a drink as the night ends while we are walking along the main [the inbetween is still missing from pub to road] road after having a tank full of drinks to rescue his son Cole from boarding school. *I call it Hogwarts. He* texted Jonny upset, begging him to bring him home so I piped up: "let's rescue him". We arrived at the school. e gates being closed and locked Jonny climbs over the black iron gates inside there's a sensor so the gates start opening before me, standing on the outside Jonny looks back "hurry up before they shut again."he whispers as to not wake the school kids sleeping in the building nearby. *And what a beautiful school that was.* " how'd you do that .. magic..? As the gates swing open ", everything felt like Hogwarts. is school was Hogwarts. *Clearly not but it made me laugh.* There were lovely plants placed directly below each pillar of each classroom as we walked along the gravel school grounds .. we quietly walk by the *Som* building, *classes named after someone I suppose*?

By this point Cole comes down and sneaks out by the black iron fire escape iron spiral staircase from the top of the stunning Queen Victoria style,era, building. It was extremely high up, nonetheless I don't like heights. is was similar looking just like the one from the movie ree Men and a little lady, the school [love that film].. So pretty.. So Jonny has me walking around through tall perfectly cut hedge pathways and past a barn converted into a music studio, then up by the Con building as we turn around we go back finding ourselves climbing the iron stairway to the point I can't recall making it to the top. Did I black out by this point? .. .. the next thing I remember is waking up in Jason Dingos back seat as he peers round and says hi with a big grin on his face as Jonny had called him out of a nice sleep by the looks of his sticking up hair to come rescue us three, yes we rescued Cole he wanted to go home and see his daddy, bless him.. So sitting up in Jason's range rover, or discovery I'm not sure a big 4x4 nevertheless. Coles in the front Jonny in the back I'm in the back to the right Jonny always sits on the left. It's weird. I notice this and in bed he sleeps on the right . (*my memory is tossed about like fkn miracas*).. Upon waking I slowly sit up and lean forward to see Jason as he leans round. ~Hey, remember me? *Omg ru having a laugh that's the entire plot problem,* as if, I had met him load of times in pubs he came introduced himself and the shouting at me when I was taking a innocent walk in the countryside he didn't know I had amnesia, and I had no idea who he was or that I'd met him before too.

In fact I also saw him in his swimming trunks, which wasn't a bad thing to remember. Jason spoke: 'Ignore the state of me,' he had no eyebrows, or very blond ones and began to explain how they draw them in for him on tv. ere was at no point in that period of my recall anything anyone could have done to allow my memories to reach me which must have been as confusing for them as it was for me._is is why I keep asking how do you know my name_ ? Not once did anyone give me a clear explanation of how they knew me, they just said nothing. For that reason I leaped no further with my progress. So he drove me home and put me to bed. I just recall opening my eyes as Jason and Jonny stood over me for a split second after they returned me home safely and then I'm out like a light.

[As the floodgates are now opened at first it was a lot every day by this point it's not often at all and I don't tend to have time to process and progress any further unless something happens that I really need that information I am no longer pursuing. Which is why this is my letting go at this point via my diaries.]

These memories just come at random: and they're now this big unfolding picture.
This was my life before, this was me but how..? I need to find the right place for this memory in time.

I'm walking through a small town clearly.. when Jonny's son stops the car he hurriedly jumps out and shouting "Tabitha, come with me, come with me" quickly he's mad rushed for time and frantically he grabs me and pushes me into the back of the car and he wouldn't take no for an answer.... his driver a woman at the time I thought was his gf but I was mistaken she was a taxi driver, so we pull up at one of Jonny's houses driveways, Coles way ahead of me and rushing to run to open the front door waving his arms come on come on hurry up come in...I've been in this house a few times but as you can imagine there is nothing there familiar to me. I may as well have been in a new country. Cole calls me inside so I ask the driver to wait. I didn't want to be stuck there. I follow him into the kitchen. He's unbagging his shopping but Jonny comes in and he says he's busy today but o fers to drive me home, err no, I was actually on my way to a night out so drop me to the town my friends are at please, It also wasn't as far so better for us both... so he gives me a lift back to town on the way he said if I was single I'd like to take you out .. Am I getting an odd feeling here? He and I have deja vu. These meetings are becoming too frequent . Cole had told me how much he hated Jonny's girlfriend (not his wife, side chick)and how he knows his dad loves me, please come and see my dad please he loves you Tabitha.[*he meant love like a good friend*] Why is this kid playing cupid? I'm really confused at this stage who his dad is, so weird. What a sweet thing to say, and I'd forgotten him too but it was only months apart I'd seen him too, why can't I hold onto my memories. As Jonny dropped me o f in the town square I explained what his son had said, "go spend more time with your son" . He sounds like he needs more of your attention and Jonny nodded. 'Yea I know I will,and thanks for listening to him'. I added: "and one to one with him don't be introducing him to lots of side chicks he doesn't want to see that." So there's me giving him a lecture and from my perspective he's a stranger and from his side he knew me. Who is this lad's dad ? I can't remember him either at this time. I'm lucky that I just go with the flow in life and take day by day moment by moment and let these things go over like water o f a duck's back. Not once did I go to see my dr and mention this until five years ago and look that turned out to be ine fective.

So I've known some of these people my entire life. ere is a family I still can't recall. I've had them try to speak to me over the years and I still can't fit their faces into place just yet. Will I ever be able to or is this it or will there be more to come I just don't know yet. ere are too many random ones, even Jonny dressed up with big fake noses so as not to be recognised in bars he made himself look unattractive so he could sneak in undetected.. One night on the way home from the bar he was wheeling himself in a wheelchair on my route home, he see me coming up behind him along the road on foot, he turns round and looks, he's startled by it being me, I o fered to push him he then pulled o f a fake nose threw it in the hedge along the side of the road hops out pulls his trouser legs down as he had them rolled up to look disabled. He grabs the chair and throw it in the hedge and laughs I'll get that tomorrow, as we walk along the road we sit on a bench and talk a while we hadn't seen each other in a long time it felt, but this was before that head injury when I had him fixed as a mate while we were always randomly picking each other up we'd both regularly hitchhike I did as I loved being free and walking the roads was my thing. Over the years he gave me cars or sorted one out for me within the same day, if I said I don't have one, well actually, He once walked with me miles to a garage to get me a car, then vanished o f into thin air like he had to go somewhere.

There was one club with a secret entrance through a fridge door as we climbed through this club all eyes on us.. He would then switch Coleal and hide, he would be all loving and attentive when nobody could see and as soon as there was an audience he turned and ran. ere was times I would say to him as we got ready to head out to a club " I'm on the pull tonight, I'll help you find a woman you help me find a man" I was young and had no ambitions to settle down any time soon, freedom was the goal hit the road with one bag and not be tied down with a single thing._____This was my dream.

Little did I know I would end up with a large family of children. Little did I know I would end up having to deal with the loss of two of his babies down the line in years to come.

Chapter Four

I've reached my thirties. I had a happy life and as this went on in time I began to love it, I was on top of the world, I had good savings, wanted for nothing, a new car every year well new to me but a newish one anyway. ings were pretty good. I had my children, then I got married and divorced pretty soon, too young to really deal with the commitment, that drive to be free was always rooted within me to be alone, after all I was alone all my life so I became used to this and found comfort that way. My hobbies were what was the drive within me, enjoying that creative side I had within me all along due to being pretty good at art there wasn't much one couldn't take on. Academically speaking was where some confidence was lacking it held me back to trying new things .. Outer pressures made me dig in my heels more. Once I was left to my own devices I was creeping forward and intrepidly taking on said challenges. Woodwork was my favorite. I had an eye for beauty in furniture but never the funding to own it. Learning how to recreate this was the only way I'd ever own anything really nice. I am out right against wasting money and being frugal always because we were a poor family luxury didn't surround me. If I spend so much time alone I may as well surround myself with beautiful furniture. is didn't really stick if I'm honest as being poor meant soon as I created something others liked it would sell from under me, this helped my lifestyle and enabled me to give my kids the best toys for christmas growing up and wonderful day trips out to the zoo or a random lets go to Ireland in the early hrs we'd get up hit the road and travel across the Irish sea to visit friends and family.. e dream was to buy a little Irish cottage one day. Not really sure at my age now whether it's realistic or ever to happen. But dreams are what makes us keep moving forward.

There was a time I used to be romantically minded before I grew up and realized that isn't the real world at all. We used to wander round the river banks locks or even take boats out down the river ames Jonny and I. His boats or we'd borrow one from others. Everyone had a boat in those days. I said one day I always see boats with names but I never see my name on them. A week later he invited me along for a walk as we crossed the lock bridge he pointed over look there's was a boat with my name.. is was exciting for me but as I turned away he waved his arm and the guy on the boat pulled the sticker o f and under it was another name. I looked at him. I wasn't sure to be mad or laugh that he'd gone to the trouble the thought was there at least. He would keep asking what do you want to do, what are your dreams and every single one of them was fulfilled.

One weekend He took me to Paris to a recording studio. I was just following behind him going into a room with all gold records framed on a wall.. We'd been in the pubs all day. We were no way near sober in fact I believe we drank all the way from our village to France, as a result woke up in Paris. e man in the studio put his hands on my shoulders asking me, "Do you want to be a singer ?" no, my reply no. that's not my dream at all Jonny grabs me by the hand and runs me into another room. What are you doing why turn down this chance.. I don't want to be famous, I'm shy, I'm scared of crowds. I hated when he took me places nad big crowds looking at us taking photos terrified me. We'd run. *and Imean I ran for my life it felt.*

Being we just had copious amounts to drink, I'm saying we were silly, young and foolish and 'he' had this stupid idea to photocopy our asses in this o fice room. He did it first then he lifted me up and as I landed I broke the glass. *Our faces as we heard the smash was total oh shit* At this moment the man walked in having a go at us. Jonny is hiding behind him while he's looking at the print of my bare butt photo.. is moment felt like forever and I wanted the ground to open up and swallow me whole. Jonny's eyes went really big as he gazed upon it.. Omg we ran out of there laughing and red faced after a brief telling o f.

We caught a bus to the Ei fel Tower, again crowds of people seemed to surround us. It was su focating. He was used to it and I wasn't comfortable. Being used to not seeing a soul for days in the village life crowds and towns were not my thing. We go up to the cafe in the top, I look around and say something like "well that's disappointing." I thought it was posh. It felt like a cafe like any cafe except for the view that was nice. e young lad who worked there laughed at my response as I covered my mouth then lowered my hand. Sorry I don't mean it, my mouth works before my brain kicks in and this happens a lot and it makes me extremely unpopular more than often._I actually think it's the most romantic thing anyone has ever done for me.

He was like a best friend. We were so comfortable around each other. He saw me at my worst and my best but it didn't bother me how he saw me. I wasn't after him in that way .. he was too fickle and always running o f .. 'I can't be seen with you' he'd say.. I said 'but you have been seen with me many times so stop being a drama queen you fkin idiot.' He got used to the brash things I'd say to put him in place. We walked around and he showed me the beach where we swam out to this floating platform he said come on let's go for a swim and I stripped down to what I thought was my thong and bra to swim in but it vanished once it got wet he was trying to cover me..I recall I was chatting to this french man who swam over to join us. He was trying to explain to me how to pronounce the town in french but could I get a handle on this .. no could I hell I can hardly speak well in english let alone french. We walked along the town I even loved the letter boxes why did I say that looking back at Jonny's face he was laughing you love this town too he asked me," I love it I want to live here" I replied he said that's how I felt too when I first came here, it was beautiful .. it must have been the town he has a house in as everyone knew him. is confused me when they spoke to me in french I kept looking back at Jonny confused how drunk am I everyone sounds funny. . . this had him bursting out in laughter, we're in Paris you idiot ? I never heard him laugh so much in fact he wouldn't let it drop all day. I felt like pushing him into the sea by the end.

We ended up in a supermarket and he marched o f ahead. Are you hungry? grab something, I wasn't, I suggested beers so the party didn't stop all weekend.

Suddenly it's the middle of the night, I awoke in a medium sized bedroom with an ensuite, to our right was a narrow window looking down into the street below. e walls were warmly plain painted net curtains and heavy main curtains to which I jumped up to go open. I liked the location of this hotel. It felt so warm I didn't want to leave it . I think Jonny had a man carry me up. We had so much to drink. "Wow I love this room Jonny" he sits up and shouts 'go back to sleep' he never liked being woken, always grumpy unless he wakes up naturally then it's always his terms and most of the time he wakes up horney. He taught me things I only ever did with him, never with anyone else he was demanding that way but I wasn't willing to try it again with anyone else.

He'd try so hard to give me my dreams, he took me to the Tate Gallery to show me a painting of a woman with eyes just eyes and part nose he said Tabitha that's you do you like it ? I thought he was kidding and laughed was my reply.. I always said the wrong thing trying to be facetious which always backfired. We were so drunk it all started sitting on the roadside bank of long grass talking at ten am one saturday morning about dreams, and within minutes he said run in grab your passport now and that was it we hit the road on the tunnel to France..

On the way home we had to grab a private jet he had to film the next day at eleven am he'd forgotten because of the great time we were having, shit, shit, he said turning his head left to right we got to go, we had a driver take us to the airport and private jet I was in and out of sleep the worst hangover in the world was about to kick in. As we landed in town close to where we lived he had a driver take me home and he shot o f to work at the studios. I was sick and didn't turn up for work for a week. A few days later he dropped o f my passport at my door and handed it to my mum. He was told she's ill, but he took this as rejection.

I saw him two weeks later he found me in a nearby town in England hanging out with friends he ran over "where have you been I've been looking for you" I said go away I don't know why I said that, the feeling to just snap at him exploded and his eyes filled up as he turned heels ran o f, he stopped turned around give me one filthy look and said I've met someone else in the last two weeks anyway.

I couldn't be bothered to argue we weren't a couple anyway we were only ever fun buddies/old friends. e agreement was mates, I'd find a man he'd find a woman. ere was a time we woke up in my caravan while cooking breakfast and during a row over how to cook eggs, he flipped my egg over and I wanted it runny and the look of how dare you he had from me his face was fearful.. " if we don't marry by the time we are fourty we should marry each other " I joked .. he was already in a relationship, and a stupid line from a movie I would blurt them out time to time and he hated it. As he was about to leave he closed the door looking back at me deep in thought~ cu later!.. I think that was the last time I had a memory of ever knowing who he was. I *have a memory bank full of waking with him in all of my houses by now and I in his houses.*

In reflection these attacks left me with limited memories and ability to hold onto some things new too, *of course there's more to it than just the skull*

fractures but I feel the need to leave out the negative parts in the book before, this is a sequel of course.. you don't miss what you never had. What you don't know doesn't bother you is the only way to explain it.

I did find it odd this man with long hair kept turning up at places I and mean places plurally. While I was in LA I decided to leave my motel and go for a walk to look around. e weather was lovely, just how I liked it warm enough to wear a t shirt and skirt but not too humid. Suddenly a voice from across the road said "Tabitha"? As I peer across the street 'hi Tabitha' do you want me to show you around ?..holding out his arms in the direction of the town toad he was walking along.. ' no,thank you' (I had no idea who he was still) 'I'm married'. I replied and he looked down and made an 'argh' sound of disappointment as I waved my ring like it was a final goodbye. I had no idea how he knew my name.. is kept happening for thirty one years. I now have a diary full of his "hello Tabitha" from him in my memory bank of this man. Each time we meet he is a total stranger all over again, admittedly thus each time we meet I would ask "HOW DO YOU KNOW MY NAME?", he would make a waving downwards movement with his arms and walk away like he was convinced I was playing him for a fool..even though I would stand there bewildered by this as he walked away I'd then think to myself maybe he thinks I'm someone else shrug this o f and move on with my day and with my life. . Sometimes he tried to tell me to please remember him but it made no sense at all, there was nothing to access within me as much as I tried I had to wait for it to come naturally back.

Flowers would be delivered and when I say flowers I mean gigantic baskets and bouquets over the years gifts would be delivered at the door. I never understood even Valentine cards signed J. I wasn't sure this was his mind for sure but the flowers he always left a card with his name but this name meant nothing to me. I couldn't recall it even though I knew it from before the attacks. He painted me this beautiful painting of a baby elephant. e paint was still wet, he came into my house the painting wrapped in crepe paper he made me a cup of tea and told me to put my feet up I was heavily pregnant, talking to me like he knew me but I was just thinking he's a friendly delivery driver and I didn't understand the gift. On the back it read, Tabitha, in the grass, against a wall, along the road, in the trunk, in my bed alone. 'I shouldn't have left you alone', he said, as he walked out my door after handing me the painting . Before he left he asked if he could feel the baby kick. . As it was the last week before I was due as she kicked he jumped backwards and shot across the room in fright as if the kick booted him across and I had to laugh but I still didn't understand why he was there.

When my first son was born[my first born] he was there waiting in the corridor for me, when I took him to register him. Jonny appeared and wanted to come with me to the registry o fice, in fact he appeared just as I was about to enter the building. He kept turning up for my pregnancy scans. I can't recall him ever missing one now but there were many over the years..me he was always a stranger each time. He was there at three of my children's births, in fact he cut the cord of two. I just presumed he was a volunteer always at hospitals and thought no more of it but every so often I'd look back and catch him looking sad at me, I would shrug it o f and carry on with my life and that moment was lost all over again.

It wasn't just him it was a lot more than that but others just called me scatty and spent enough time around me to be imprinted etched in my life as a part of it in some form. Sometimes I would think I'd seen someone last week and I hadn't seen them for months so that was odd but I soon adapted this to my scatty memory and it really didn't matter as I keep a daily diary of events and bookings for if I have to meet anyone it's there now. I began to keep a diary during some of the attacks. At one point I wrote on a notepad before I went to bed how this person isn't nice and in the morning I can recall thinking why was this written down and progress from there was made. ese notes began to be my cued recall. I would trust myself, trusted my word from the day before of how someone was and the next day begin to wean away realizing I no longer need undesirables around me as in people who were gaslighting me this didn't help my recall I could only rely upon myself as it was soon to light others had ulterior motives they knew what was missing they knew about Jonny but they lied to me when I asked them for help they'd keep me in the dark as it worked out better for them that way.

There's a time I took life less for granted and began to walk away, finally finding how much happier this made me feel in doing so, keeping only those close to me I trusted and having a meaningful small circle walking by my side.

To the best of my knowledge I don't think it's all recalled yet but that's ok if it stays buried . Others too tried to reach out to me, there were moments when Jonny's mother would try to tell me, she was a lot older now and more frail than I'd ever seen her before. She even tried to get me to go on a date with him once but I declined being heavily pregnant finding this odd at the time. His father even tried to speak to me,[*he was a strong rugged man,]* about the baby, and his older brother even tried to get through to me for some reason. I always remembered him though oddly perhaps he slipped into the time period of which a few memories stayed grounded? *ey both looked like their grandfather on the mothers side* Obviously Jonny was upset somehow and he had told his family but I was in the dark about what I'd done. *(the abortion) that is why he was mad and rightly so.)*

I adjusted to thinking people are mean and having a bad day, until all the memories came back it all began to slip into a clarity in form … each piece fitted alongside another odd memory I had to patch together like a jigsaw until it came to light. I still have a few memories that I don't have a time period for and even faces I don't yet know. I can't recall years yet but I recall where it was and who was there, if I get a rough idea of how old my children are in the memories. I can narrow it down to a year in winter or summer at this point which is pretty good considering there was nothing before that for years. Old photos help now too at looking at the back for dates or items of furniture or how the room was laid out this solves a lot of missing pieces.

New beginnings is probably the best thing to do keeping that diary.. I believe whatever it was that was broken is now healed and for some or whatever reason the memories have come back there is nothing I can do but laugh at the funny moments of my youth and remember not to lose myself along the way. I have a grandchild on the way at this stage in life so there will always be something to keep busy. I still have that life goal of owning my own home one day. Bringing out the best in me remembering who I used to be has been such fun. Even Ryan Goose turned up to my baby's birth to demand a dna test along with Jonny Stepp the same day. Imagine that as your life memories .. that was some party I'll never forget ~again !

Chapter Five

There were periods in the early days of the crazy sex life that we had, from having made out in places from a list that hadn't been done yet, you name it we did it, even tried to do it on a motorbike but we fell o f.

On the roof of a village hall and got caught by the press, and in the back of car after he paged the radio to play tacky romance songs as we sat in the layby, to side of the road in the grass, on a beach, up against a wall to the trunk of a car inside door closed while being given a lift to his place.

One of the cued recalls was seeing him have a interview on TV chat show of him talking about this moment and other moments he mentioned me driving my mini eight of us inside where I had it on two wheels, he mentioned the new year kiss we shared in 1995 when Kath Myer got mad at me for taking her kiss at midnight they had to repeat their shoot at one thirty am.

That night we agreed to do a photo shoot in a champagne bath but I fell asleep of course then I pulled the plug after I felt how cold and sticky it was.

Wanting to do this shoot with my dress on which was black, the stockingings were a sheen denier which at this point I wanted o f so I could be comfortable but the photographer wanted me to take o f all my clothes so Jonny and I were expected to climb into this cold drink .. brr. I thought better of it and went to sleep in his and Kaths hotel room. To be honest it wasn't much of a nice hotel, a bit dingy to be honest and disappointing compared to other places I'd stayed. During this exhausthing moment of sleep I'm nudged and awoken to Kath and Jonny having fits of laughter laying on each side of me in the hotel bed with the photos being taken there instead with me fast asleep and them two doing di ferent positions around me in fits. I think Kath fell o f the bed laughing so hard at one point. I liked Kath only meeting her briefly in the bar earlier that evening. We chatted a bit. Laughing about one of her ex's and how unsuited he was but he wasn't a bad looking fella.

Oddly one that didn't leave my mind was Pete Decor.. Although he wasn't there that evening I hit it o f with Pete years before, he even took me home to his mum's once, what did I end up doing, I fell up his stairs soon as I walked in the door what a great first meet impression, drinking with these people is something I don't do well as I'm five beers and asleep. But recall being fond of Pete. I felt a connection with him..forgetting my life including Kath, Ryan, Martin, and Charlie for years meaning having met them and laughed meeting them upon sleep the mind wipes out the day or part of the day before at least the inadequacy of being able to hold onto these moments in time. Unexpectedly times and dates alongside life experiences are running around in my mind swirling like a magnet rolling on a metal sphere without having a place to grip or assimilate to where it belongs briefly mystifying against all odds after twenty six years it begins to slow down and find a placement to settle.. Meanwhile, is it really needed? After all these years I found myself doing perfectly fine without them. ey can just sit on the shelf of one's memory bank at this stage and probably be left there and never mentioned again. Perhaps the odd flashback will bring a smile to my face like the time spent with Vinny Sinc two nights of seeing him on a night out in row. He kissed me but there was others in the room so we had no privacy but I do remember feeling his muscles under the duvet. Well now I do Is it me or is my world getting smaller all of a sudden.

Amnesia is apparently unresolving, from what I read but it's not forever in some cases. ere's no specific way to resolve the fact the brain can no longer hold onto new memories or find it di ficult to keep hold of new, but diaries could seemingly be healthy to promote this trigger of memory recall. at's why this is being written there is no way of knowing these unforgettable moments in time will not be wiped once more so to have this down on paper is to be a safety net to fall back upon if all is lost once more as old age progresses.

The uncertainty of what the future will hold, not to take for granted the future or expect these memories are here and back for good, how easily they were taken and how five years to regain remembrance is this the beginning of losing it all or is it here to stay? Cognitively things seem ok, even new skills learned along with new challenges have been undertaken.

As the feeling washes over me yet again in a flash I find myself sitting on the rivers bank and something familiar as I look across the river there is a woodpecker in a cluster of trees, how beautiful I feel deja vu coming over me. As this triggers this memory but I don't figure how ther'ye connected at this moment until later.

Jonny took me to Helena Rivers house (an actress) She was I believe a comedian, she was young at the time then I must have gone way back with this memory. I'm a very young woman, and somehow I ended up sitting at her kitchen table. I recall being vetted for information as to why J and I were friends and at that time we were innocent friends in a way most of the time.

I liked her home and she was welcoming. ere were others there too at the table, some names yet to come back to me... years went by when she approached me again while out in a pub, she walked over. I think she was holding a stick. If I recall correctly, she's shorter than me, it feels in my memory she was looking up slightly and she could have been wearing flats. I could have been in heels that would have given an illusion of this too, also she's very pretty. After complimenting her on this the conversation was short lived. Jonny says across the crowded bar 'hi' waving, as Helena is talking to me, I reply how do you know my name, this confuses her too, she looked concerned at Jonny then he whispered to her. I'm wondering now did he know I had lost every memory of the past we ever had together, I couldn't even remember meeting her either. She probably was confused as It was five years ago when this deviating loss has turned itself back around and returned to its original state and settled itself into my left side of the brain which explains how terrible I am at math perhaps.

How Do You Know My Name?

Did I lose any other skills along this puzzling path of life, hoping there is some wonderful skill I would have preowned that may come along with it, but in hindsight of losses for that reason it appears unfortunately unlikely.

As I'm still reflecting upon my life of fifty years, *halfway to a hundred who knew I'd make it this far.*.I recall meeting Brian Wells (a singer) in a local town when we were young. He stopped to say hello, all the makeup was on him as we passed in the exact same spot years before the Jonny kiss on the same curb. His hair was short then spiked on top with the overuse of gel and hairspray. e foundation on him was thick with his lips in dark lipstick, in those days I used to believe if a man wore make-up he was a cross dresser if I'm honest. Who knew today's society being just that in addition to this he was ahead of us all. He stopped, said hello briefly, chatted and o fered a photo to which my reply was no. .I'm in a hurry, I was on my way into the shop to grab something for that evening ahead and I wanted to go home to get ready. It was a nice sunny day but I can't tell you what time of year it was, spring perhaps.. I wasn't one to be all star struck and needing the photo thing, he did tell me who he was he seemed to want to talk longer I got that vibe. He was super friendly.

..Months passed the flash backs would come uninvited day or night but mostly when I was resting and there was a quiet moment to relax, I suppose I keep incredibly busy most of the time so I don't stop and dwell to think back if ever being honest these are not particularly wanted memories it's like they're being purposely shown to me by my own mind as a kick up the arse to learn by it. *e memories have come back for a reason but I haven't figured out yet what that reason is.* I digress bare with me:

Years before meeting Fred Minster (he was a pop star very popular in the 70's)he had gel slicked hair, skin tight jeans and a silk shirt undone to see his hairy chest, in those days he was a sexy symbol but being nieve I hadnt must familiarity that there was such a thing as gays I really did lead a sheltered life so when a friend turned and said lovers quarrel I didnt get it. I was only fifteen. Shouldn't have been there but we were pretending to be older drinking snake bites which was a half and half mix of larger and cider. ose drinks ended up being banned as it made everyone so drunk and aggressive they had to put pay to that phase. I heard him say I'm tired too. I just drove three and half hours to come see you and had an argument in the middle of the night and now I have to drive all the way back at this time. He then turned to look at me as I was watching and listening the entire time and said 'do you want a picture'? I thought he was being sarcastic so I replied 'no thanks', but he meant an actual photo. I was young and presumed he was derisive.

My most treasured memories were probably Charlie lynch at his house and meeting Tom Warner (actor) at the air show the day I had drove Jonny there, to which he abandoned me and I collapsed with heat stroke. It was a heatwave that day and I wasn't well. But I didn't make a hash of meeting Tom, ok maybe I did. He was the only person I actually jumped for joy to meet and getting a 'hi Tabitha' I shout 'love you' he replied immediately ' love you Tabitha' *like he would say to all his fans I almost fainted in aw and wave was the bomb.* I said a few other silly things. It wouldn't be me if I didn't slip up saying something inappropriate.

Who's to say this won't be lost again, how do I know how long my memory will keep it this time,, is it back for good, why didn't I remember so many times in the past, but I guess there is an explanation now in spite of it all it finally makes sense ? *books* One won't make sense without the other.

Reading through old notes I found out that Ryan Goose he ended up having a DNA test with one of my babies, the nurse handed me two DNA tests from him, one from Jonny. As I left I took them home for the baby's paperwork as her medical records. ey were done on a portable printer they paid £500.00 each for a test they were printed on long thin strips not like you'd expect it to be printed. Jonny had paid for me to have a private room. He came for three days in a row and fed the baby, dressed her and took care of her while I recovered from a c'section. Yet when the midwife came to visit me she asked me about him and I said I have no idea what you're talking about. I'm sorry ?_IT WAS GONE! I heard Jonny in the hallway say it's only been three days but i'm already in love with her' *I think he meant the baby.* Looking through my baby photos years later I discovered a photo of him in my room. is was a small trigger to start to recall but it didn't come for a few years still even with the pictures. You can't force a memory to come back. All you can do is wait and try to move on with the present time. If it doesn't come back it's no loss. '**You can't miss whatyou don't know you once had.**'

This is my real life fairytale e most gentleman of all gentlemen was Prince Louis. Now I'm not saying he was a perfect gentleman because where's the fun in that but .. But as a respectful man he stayed with me all night. We sat in my car. He even brought me a glass of water, [1]including giving me his jumper to keep as a keepsake. I met him through Peter (he was a millionaire nightclub owner) he had long hair in a pony tail gray which later on took the elastic out for photos. He wore a suit jacket if I recall correctly. e same night I met him in fact, I was driving Louis home from this club and as I spun the car around outside string-cards the club in london to head back in the opposite direction there was Sid (a soap actor) he waving us o f outside as I drove us away shouting 'go Tabitha, go, yessss' his arms shot up in the air like a big hurray.. cheers came from all who watched this unfold outside the club. I had met sid earlier in the club I was the most annoying person to him that night I think I said three times 'RICHY' shouted his stage name as his stage wife character it got tiresome but I do push limits when i'm having a laugh but he just looked at me like i've heard this so many times before please its gotten old. But I still did it and then eventually got a big smile from him in the end.

I made a promise to him as it could be catastrophic, but everything has already been catastrophic so why shouldn't I have that one good thing to hold close as it brings heartwarming comfort to look back at now i'm old and to recall such a wow moment is exactly what the dr ordered. As we drive along the roads we passed the Black Cabs and he was explaining to me what they were for as I was overwhelmed by how many there were because after all i'm a country girl, he was telling me where to go I was afraid I would get lost but he reassured me all the way giving directions... After I spin the car around a few times in a circle we were having such fun laughing, he got worried at first but soon realized I was messing around and relaxed, so we eventually pull up next to a curb, we had already driven under a arch where a guard was pointing us to go but Louis shouted up it's just me its ok and he told me carry on so I did, I pull the car alongside a curb there were low hedges neatly cut.. ere's a path to my left, a longish one that went into a kitchen door to the left. After an hour of chatting and whatnots, Louis invited me into Buckingham Palace where I met Her Majesty Queen Elizabeth and Prince Charles, it being the middle of the night they were both dressed for bed.. And His Majesty Prince Arthur wasn't happy to see me at that hour; that wasn't how I would have predicted meeting him at all. In the club I wore a black dress, Louis pranked me then kissed me, Paul Stringfellow took photos of us. I made a promise and I think I owe him that much to say no more on that subject without the details at least.. 'Perfect' is all I can say about him, how amazing he was. He was raised properly with manners and dignity, I can't say a single thing I would change about him. I may add this isn't a list of comparisons All are equal, all are in one amazing memory called life.

My world is getting smaller and smaller

Chapter Six

I'd like to address the last five years, which haven't been easy but they have been peaceful. Money hasn't been as good which is why I now work two jobs and even then I can't a ford a holiday or a car of my own. I rely on a company car for one of my jobs which I guess I should be grateful for ~'count your blessings not your sorrows' they say. e children are all grown up now, almost bar one. Life takes peaks and turns in directions you wouldn't believe. I had omas Hill[another big movie star] scream and swear in my face in a bar, he did apologize, I haven't a clue why, Sakura [Jonny's new gf] and Jonny came to my defense, to top it o f that evening I had Ryan Goose kissing me on the cheek in a bar but at the time I hadn't a clue or had the memory of him by then, he said I owed you a kiss, we were disturbed that night years ago before we even got to have a kiss I recall that now as the jigsaw pieces fell and locked in place...

My life was now flowing faster than ever all in one big final pile of boxes just chucked at me, methodically a box of memoirs. I find myself sitting in the middle of a cafe and my mind wanders o f to the past yet again. I recall meeting Adrian Bowen(Tv entertainer) in a town where he has a shop for home design. I guess as we passed he said you know me?

I looked trying to find that memory of this man who had the biggest smile on his face as we were passing in the town shopping center, looking back at one another in deep thoughts trying to rekindle where and when but couldn't put a finger on it.. do I laughing he kept looking back yes you do, I had met him years ago but those two moments all flooding back this last five years has been odd to say the least. at was just a hi in a busy bar but it came back the smallest meet in my mind came back too. Day by day I was remembering lost relatives and lost lovers. e strangest part of it was how I was carrying on until now, especially cognitively. Daily events did not go, learning how to cook didn't go or riding a bike or driving a car all those things never left.. How is amnesia even a thing? Misplaced memories in my case.

There's a few more names to add to the list I suppose, the night Cole White sneaked from his boarding school into a local town pub he was plied with drink sitting in the corner by the window he said something to me but I can't recall a brief hi perhaps 'he wasn't famous then but somehow my memory is handing it all on a plate like sitting in front of a screenplay watching your life reel out in front of you for the first time all over again, but of course reassuringly I know what I'm recalling is my life story. Tony Het I met as I gate crashed Georgo Partin's party, Paul Dandol [magician] I met while he was on stage I was called out in the audience to ask a question. I had another fond memory of a member from a band called BUGS, he was so sweet to meet, in fact I now hold them all dear. Little flashbacks of Ryan trying to make me remember him at the hospital when he demanded the DNA test, he was way too good looking for someone like me so it never entered my mind we'd of once had a thing, but there's another reason for that which is still surfacing. Evan lee kirk I recall him snapping some of Jonny's photos for the paper years ago outside Jonny's Dads house down a country lane as I passed them I thumbs up to them Jonny shouts 'love you Tabitha' like he always did, and meeting lee at parties or pubs *he was in movies too same par as J*, the conversations were always odd to me they'd speak to me as if I was somebody they knew in their younger days sadly yet I had no recall of this but the familiarity of how they spoke was a memory jogger, they really helped me without even knowing it. Practically subordinating passion into reasoning myself and my life into this box. I'd rather not have any more losses thus keeping photos is fundamental. I now hold these photos dear beholding insight within my life before. Including the tattoo on my back put there by Jonny when I was a teen.

Remarkably I finally evoked who was within me.

I was a Model. If It wasn't for stumbling across my pictures on social media with the roll call of names to my surprise. To my consternation this sparked something inside_'I think that's me?'

On reflection, If someone asks you, 'how do you know my name?' tell them, even briefly, you never know you may rekindle something.

The End

Threequel peek

With this new knowledge and secrets that Tabitha possesses she finds herself protecting them for their safety, after all they took care of her, now it's her turn to look after them. is secret world that only exists within the realms of their domains especially when money is involved. Now that her attackers are in prison, will other inmates be made aware of what they are?

Their peace in the nick was about to change when an undercover prison officer purposely places himself in Wandsworth prison to be close at hand. Are these criminals aware that the police now have a record of all their criminal doings? All they need now is for them to slip up, but will they accidently confess, if that maybe what nightmare is about to be unleashed? Criminal Justice comes in all shapes and forms, some call it karma. is undercover prison officer has his own personal vendetta to dealing with these types of men and it has now become very personal indeed.

Synopsis

The Book How Do You Know My Name has been written by the Author Mia Collins as a sequel to Sangfroid. This being a fictional story has been written from a different point of view unlike the third party in the first book, though written as a diary form therefore as a Fictional Autobiography. Tabitha suffered from amnesia for twenty six years, she unfurls how her forgotten life reveals itself over a period of several years. Thereafter her memories returned, unfolding her unique life she once enjoyed although sadly forgotten due to a major blow to the head leaving her in a coma for two weeks with a fractured skull. As her memories unfold it's a whirlwind of wonderful twists and turns as she finally learns who the mystery man was all along who helped her back to this point of now being fulfilled. Who was he, perhaps someone who used to be her oldest friend? who Tabitha no longer recognised.

Disclaimer

If any names or places seem familiar in real life it's purely coincidental, therefore used in a 'sound like context' to appear more powerful as a character for readers to relate to as perception for their imagination.

Milton Keynes UK
Ingram Content Group UK Ltd.
UKHW011122280124
436772UK00003BA/34/J

9 781669 890522